At Your Service

Written by

JM Sheridan

Illustrated by

Jamie Forgetta

To Karlie,

Take care, service dogs like Major G are everywhere!

Visit our website at **www.StillwaterPress.com** for more information.

First Stillwater River Publications Edition

ISBN-13: 978-1-950-33961-7

1 2 3 4 5 6 7 8 9 10

Written by JM Sheridan

Illustrated by Jamie Forgetta

Published by Stillwater River Publications, Pawtucket, RI, USA.

DEDICATION

To Brianna, my muse, my inspiration, my drive.

May you always help those in need.

To my husband, Kevin, for standing with me

and always believing in me.

To Bri and Sami Lee for your honest first read through.

Janie, I'm happy I challenge you to find your inner child.

Your poetry is beautiful.

To Jamie, for your good-hearted nature, and great illustrations.

May we work together for years to come.

To Canines for Disabled Kids. Your heart is true and in the right place.

JM Sheridan will always support your efforts.

A Special Dog

Some dogs chase cats
and play tug of war
and bark when someone
knocks on the door
Others play ball
and roll in the dirt
but I was trained
to do important work
I assist special children
who need extra help
with things they cannot
do for themselves
I can be their eyes, or ears,
their comfort, or guide
I am my child's best friend
always by their side
I'm a proud service dog
who is pleased to serve
because a happy safe life
is what my child deserves

By

Janey Coyne-Scaturro

Published on Amazon and Facebook

"WOW, WOW, WOW!"

Brianna said, as she turned around and around.

Today she is visiting the BIG kids' high school.

"This school is HUGE!" Brianna cried out.

"Brianna WATCH OUT!" She heard her mom

SHOUT.

But it was TOO late...

BUMP!   THUMP!

Brianna TRIPPED and FELL to the floor.

"Are you OK?" Brianna heard someone ask.

"I'm OK." she replied, getting up off the FLOOR.

Brianna turned to see WHAT she had tripped over.

A DOG!

"PETS are NOT allowed in SCHOOL,"

Brianna said, stating school RULES.

"TRUE," the girl agreed, "but Major G's a

SERVICE DOG," she said pointing to his VEST,

"He can go with me EVERYWHERE."

"I'm Mia," the girl said introducing herself.

"I have EPILEPSY," she explained,

"Major G is my Seizure Alert Dog."

"What is EPILEPSY?" Brianna asked, as they

walked outside to sit on the grass.

"Sometimes, for just a few minutes, my BRAIN

can't talk to my BODY," Mia explained.

"It is like, when the car radio goes fuzzy or cuts

OUT when you drive under a BRIDGE, but as soon as

you're OUT from under the bridge,

it comes back ON."

"Major G's trained to HELP me," Mia said.

"First, he's trained to CATCH me if I fall during a

SEIZURE," she explained,

"So I don't hit my HEAD."

"Second, he knows to ROLL me on my SIDE,

then go get HELP."

"Major G can also TELL when I'm about to have a

SEIZURE," Mia said proudly.

"He can SEE the FUTURE?" Brianna asked,

"AMAZING!"

"Not quite," Mia said laughing.

"He can SMELL when a SEIZURE is about to

happen," she explained.

"He's SMART!" Brianna said reaching to pet

Major G's head.

"Please DON'T pet him," Mia stopped her. "When

a service dog's VEST is on they're WORKING and

we don't want to distract them."

"BARK! BARK! BARK!"

Brianna JUMPED to her feet!

"Hello Lulu," Mia said, to the FUNNY dog.

"PLAY TIME" she said, taking off Major G's VEST.

"Lulu's his best FRIEND," Mia explained,

"When his vest is OFF, it's time to PLAY."

"If you work as hard as Major G, you need some

FUN TIME," Mia said.

"Brianna, it's time to GO," she heard her mom call.

"Thanks for all your HARD work Major G," Brianna

said. "And thanks for taking care of Mia," she added

as she waved good-bye to her new FRIENDS.

The End

Made in the USA
Lexington, KY
27 November 2019